MR. SILLY

by Roger Hargreaves

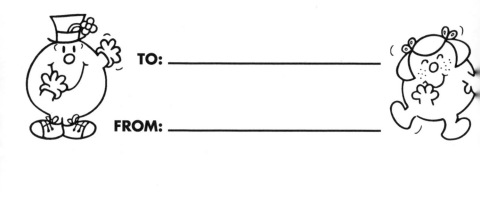

TO: _____

FROM: _____

MR. SILLY

by Roger Hargreaves

WITHDRAWN

Grosset & Dunlap

Mr. Silly lives in Nonsenseland, which is a very funny place to live.

You see, in Nonsenseland, everything is as silly as it can be.

In Nonsenseland, all the trees are red and the grass is blue!

Isn't that silly?

In Nonsenseland, dogs wear hats!

And do you know how birds fly in Nonsenseland?

No. They don't fly forward.

They fly backward!

It is really a very silly place indeed.

Which is why Mr. Silly lives there.

Mr. Silly, in fact, lives in quite the silliest-looking house you have ever seen.

Can you imagine living in a house like that?

Now, this story is all about the Nonsense Cup.

You see, each year a competition is held in Nonsenseland and the Cup is awarded to the person who has the silliest idea of the whole year.

Mr. Silly has never won the Cup, but each night, lying in his bed, he dreamed about winning it.

He realized that he would have to come up with a remarkably silly idea to win the Nonsense Cup.

Mr. Silly pondered over the problem of the Nonsense Cup one morning at breakfast.

He was having a cup of coffee with a spoonful of jelly in it.

After that, he had a cornflake sandwich.

To finish he had a boiled egg. But being Mr. Silly, he ate the shell, too!

Isn't that a silly breakfast?

Anyway, this particular breakfast time, Mr. Silly was thinking about the Nonsense Cup.

He remembered two years ago when Mr. Ridiculous won the Cup.

He won by wallpapering his house, which sounds very ordinary.

But Mr. Ridiculous wallpapered his house on the outside!

Mr. Silly also remembered last year when Mr. Foolish won the Cup.

Mr. Foolish, who was Mr. Silly's friend, had won by inventing a car.

It was quite a normal car, except for one thing. It had square wheels!

Isn't that silly?

Mr. Silly thought and thought, but it was no good. He couldn't come up with a really silly idea.

He even had another cornflake sandwich, but that didn't help, either.

So he decided to take a walk.

Off he went, leaving his front door open.

Isn't that silly?

On his walk, Mr. Silly met a chicken wearing rubber boots and carrying an umbrella.

"Wouldn't it be silly if you didn't wear rubber boots and carry an umbrella?" he asked the chicken.

"Meow!" said the chicken, because animals in Nonsenseland don't make the same noises as they do in your country.

Next Mr. Silly met a pig wearing trousers and a bowler hat.

"Wouldn't it be silly if you didn't wear trousers and a bowler hat?" he asked the pig.

"Moo!" said the pig.

Isn't that silly?

It was right in the middle of his walk that Mr. Silly got his idea.

It was a beautifully silly idea.

In fact, it was easily the silliest idea he had ever had.

He went right into town and bought a can of paint and a big paintbrush.

Mr. Silly knew he had to hurry if he was to be ready for the contest the next day!

The next day, a huge crowd gathered in the square to see who was going to win the Cup.

The King of Nonsenseland mounted the special platform and began to speak.

"Ladies and gentlemen," he said to the crowd, "it is my pleasure to award the Nonsense Cup to the person who has the silliest idea of the year."

"One of the silliest ideas of the year," continued the king, "is by Mr. Muddle the farmer. He has managed to grow a square apple!"

The crowd clapped as Mr. Muddle held up his square apple for everyone to see.

He felt sure he was going to win.

"However," said the king, "we have an even sillier idea."

Mr. Muddle's face fell.

It was a teapot entered by Mrs. Nincompoop.

It was the silliest teapot there ever was!

The crowd broke into thunderous applause.

"I therefore have great pleasure," announced the king, "in presenting the Nonsense Cup to . . ."

Just then he looked up and stopped in astonishment!

The king was looking at the tree in the middle of the square.

The tree had green leaves! Bright green leaves!

Not red leaves like all the other trees in Nonsenseland. Green leaves!

"Who did this?" cried the king.

"It was me," piped up Mr. Silly. "I painted all the leaves green last night when everyone was asleep."

Mr. Silly smiled modestly.

"A green tree!" shouted the crowd. "How silly!"

Then the king said, "This is the silliest idea I have ever seen. Therefore, I award the Nonsense Cup to Mr. Silly!"

The crowd cheered and cheered.

Mr. Silly went pink with pride.

And a bird perched high up in the silly green tree said, "Woof!" and flew off. Backward!

MR. MEN   **LITTLE MISS**

GROSSET & DUNLAP
An Imprint of Penguin Random House LLC, New York

Mr. Silly™ and copyright © 1972 THOIP (a SANRIO Company). All rights reserved. Previously
published by Price Stern Sloan, an imprint of Penguin Random House LLC. This edition
published in 2019 by Grosset & Dunlap, an imprint of Penguin Random House LLC, New York.
GROSSET & DUNLAP is a trademark of Penguin Random House LLC. Manufactured in China.

Visit us online at www.penguinrandomhouse.com.

www.mrmen.com

ISBN 9780843133523   20 19 18 17

Mr. Tickle
Mr. Greedy
Mr. Happy
Mr. Nosey
Mr. Sneeze
Mr. Bump
Mr. Snow
Mr. Messy
Mr. Topsy-Turvy
Mr. Silly
Mr. Up

Mr. Small
Mr. Daydream
Mr. Forgetful
Mr. Nervous
Mr. Noisy
Mr. Lazy
Mr. Funny
Mr. Stingy
Mr. Chatterbox
Mr. Fussy
Mr. Bou

Mr. Muddle
Mr. Dizzy
Mr. Impossible
Mr. Strong
Mr. Grumpy
Mr. Clumsy
Mr. Quiet
Mr. Rush
Mr. Tall
Mr. Worry
Mr. Non

Mr. Wrong
Mr. Skinny
Mr. Mischief
Mr. Clever
Mr. Busy
Mr. Slow
Mr. Brave
Mr. Grumble
Mr. Perfect
Mr. Cheerful
Mr. Co

Mr. Rude
Mr. Good
Mr. Nobody
Mr. Moustache
Mr. Marvelous

Mr. Adventure

$4.99 US
($6.99 CAN)

GROSSET&DUNLAP
Visit us at penguin.com/youngrea
and mrmen.com

ISBN 978-0-8431-3352-3

EAN

9 780843 133523

50499 >

31901069510610